BLACK TIGER

Zhao Lihong

Illustrated by Claudia Navarro

Little
Steps
PUBLISHING

BLACK TIGER

First published in Great Britain in 2022
by Little Steps Publishing
Uncommon, 126 New King's Rd, London SW6 4LZ
www.littlestepspublishing.co.uk

ISBN: 978-1-912678-60-0

A CIP catalogue record for this book is available from the British Library.

Translated by Jerimiah Willhite
Designed by Celeste Hulme

Printed in China
10 9 8 7 6 5 4 3 2 1

Old Juan the doorman was standing at the door of the New Leon Apartments as usual. He had one eye open and the other closed, as if he was paying close attention to every person who passed through the door, but also as if he wasn't looking at all.

Whenever anyone passed by, he would give them a robotic nod of his head. 'Hi, Juan,' they would say. 'Hello,' he would reply, then nod his head and sniff quietly.

Suddenly Old Juan's closed eye opened a little, and his face wore an expression that might have been anger or might have been joy. At the entrance to the New Leon Apartments was a little boy who was covered in dirt from his head to his toes. He had black hair and black eyes, and a very dirty face. There were bulges in his large overcoat, and he seemed to be hiding something.

'Hey, little wild thing! Where did you crawl out of this time?' called Old Juan. 'Just watch it, or else ...!'

Old Juan's tone was harsh, but the boy didn't seem scared at all. He smiled mischievously, and mimicked Old Juan by closing one eye and nodding. But the way his hands covered his bulging stomach seemed a bit strange.

Old Juan's gaze moved to the boy's hand. *What is that tucked inside his old overcoat? It keeps moving!* the doorman thought. *What is the kid up to?*

'Hey, Pedro! What's in your overcoat? You keep wriggling like a worm!'

As soon as Old Juan said that, Pedro burst out laughing. He pulled his overcoat down, and the fluffy head of a puppy popped out. It was black, and its coat was dirty – just like Pedro's face. But the pup's eyes shone with a special light, the kind that draws your eyes towards it so you can't look away. The pup lifted its head and gazed at Old Juan with an innocent expression on its little face.

Old Juan stared at the puppy for a moment. Then his tense face slackened, and a faint smile appeared. 'Where did you find that puppy?' he asked.

'In the city park. He was sick, and lying under a tree with nobody around who wanted him, so I picked him up. Let's keep him, Grandpa!' Pedro looked at the old doorman pleadingly, awaiting his answer.

'What's his name?'

Pedro blinked, then blurted out: 'Black Tiger!' He didn't even know where the name had come from. Now he hoped that the puppy could be as brave as a tiger. Black Tiger – that would be his name.

'Black Tiger? Well, that's different,' Old Juan said as he reached out and patted the dog's head. Then he gave Pedro a push towards the lobby. 'Go on! What are you waiting for?' he said. 'Find Black Tiger a place to sleep!'

Pedro cheered as he sprinted into the apartment building. Black Tiger fell out of his overcoat and onto the ground, then shook himself and ran off. After a minute, he stopped and turned to look at Old Juan, letting out two barks that echoed around the lobby.

'There's something different about that pup,' Old Juan muttered, as he watched Black Tiger and saw his shiny eyes.

Old Juan would never have said no to Pedro keeping Black Tiger. Years before, Pedro had been living on the streets – just like Black Tiger had been. Old Juan had brought Pedro home and raised him as his grandson. The two of them relied on each other, and Pedro had filled the elderly man's lonely life with joy. Now their family had two more pairs of legs, and it wasn't a bad thing at all.

The towering New Leon building was one of the largest apartment blocks in Mexico. Pedro's apartment was probably the smallest and most cramped in the whole building. It was on the ground floor and had been made just for the doorman.

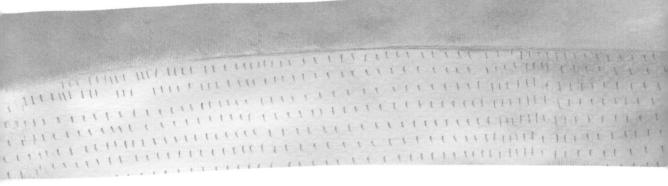

One day, Pedro asked his grandpa, 'How many people live in our building?'

His grandfather thought about it for a while. 'Who knows?' he finally answered. 'But there's got to be at least 10,000 people.'

What does 10,000 people look like? Pedro thought. Pedro was only eight years old and he could not grasp such a large number. He pointed to a flock of pigeons in Aztec Square and asked, 'Is it more than those pigeons?'

His grandpa looked at the pigeons with one eye open and the other closed. With a wave of his hand, he answered, 'It's much, much more than that!'

Wow! 10,000 people must be so many people! Pedro thought. *If they were pigeons, they would fill up the whole sky!*

Of the 10,000 people in the building, young Pedro only recognised a handful, and he only knew the names of three or four. There was José on the second floor, who was a disagreeable boy with a freckled face; there was Arturo on the third floor, who was a full head taller than Pedro; and there was Alex, a spoilt boy who limped when he walked. Pedro knew who they were for one reason – all three boys had a dog.

José's father was a policeman and he had a tall, mighty wolfhound. When José took the dog for a walk, he always stuck out his stomach and looked up towards the sky, like he was a police officer himself. Arturo had a snow-white sheepdog, which was rumoured to be a purebred Dutch shepherd – a famous, valuable breed. As for Alex, there was always a short, stocky pug at his heels which liked to bark at nothing in particular.

Pedro was jealous of these boys because they owned dogs. But they were all from wealthy families, and they didn't think of Pedro as a friend. Whenever they showed up, Pedro would try to talk with them and make friends, but they ignored him.

Once, while they were out walking, having fun with each other's dogs, they had mocked Pedro. 'You want to own a dog too? Ha! In your dreams!'

When Pedro took Black Tiger into his apartment, he felt like he was the king of the world. *I'll show you all! I have a dog too!* he thought. *But where should he put Black Tiger's bed? Right next to his own bed,* he decided. Pedro patted Black Tiger's back, saying, 'Here, Black Tiger. You can sleep here, okay?' Black Tiger seemed to understand. After a moment's hesitation, he carefully laid down and wagged his tail, as if to say, 'I love my new home!'

Pedro thought it was odd that this puppy seemed to be able to understand human speech. When he had first seen him in the park, he had waved at him and said softly, 'Come here, little pup.' The puppy had

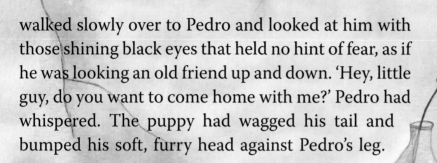

walked slowly over to Pedro and looked at him with those shining black eyes that held no hint of fear, as if he was looking an old friend up and down. 'Hey, little guy, do you want to come home with me?' Pedro had whispered. The puppy had wagged his tail and bumped his soft, furry head against Pedro's leg.

He hadn't struggled at all when Pedro had picked him up.

Now, as Pedro sat on the floor and played happily with Black Tiger, he heard someone chuckling behind him. He turned around and saw a freckled face at the door. It was José. He must have heard Black Tiger's barking at the entrance of the building and come to take a closer look.

'Hey, Pedro, where did you get that puppy?' José asked with a devilish grin. When Pedro didn't answer, he asked more seriously, 'Is a wild puppy like that even a real dog?'

'What do you think he is if he's not a dog?' Pedro snapped, glaring at José with fire in his eyes.

'Hmm, I wonder ...' José scowled. Before José could finish speaking, Black Tiger was rushing towards the door. José froze and Black Tiger's teeth clamped down on his hand.

José cried out, startled, and ran towards the stairs. 'Just you wait, wild puppy! Just you wait!' he cried.

Pedro kept laughing until tears ran down his cheeks. It was only after he'd finished laughing that he noticed Black Tiger lying quietly next to him, with his head tilted to gaze up at him with pride. He still had one of José's gloves in his mouth. It was lucky José had been wearing gloves, otherwise he might have been injured.

The next day was Sunday. The weather was fine, and Pedro took Black Tiger out for a walk. Aztec Square was filled with people and laughter. With Black Tiger trotting behind him, Pedro felt confident and important. The night before, he and his grandpa had given Black Tiger a bath to wash the dirt off, and had discovered that the pup's coat was actually brown with specks of black. Now it glistened in the sunlight. Whenever he noticed anyone looking at Black Tiger, Pedro felt very proud.

Suddenly, a bloodcurdling howl rang out behind Pedro. Pedro turned around, and what he saw stunned him. José's big dog had leapt out from somewhere and tackled Black Tiger to the ground. Now it was viciously biting Black Tiger. Black Tiger was no match for the wolfhound – all he could do was struggle in vain and yelp furiously. José was laughing triumphantly nearby, and Arturo and Alex were laughing with him.

Just as Pedro rushed forward to help Black Tiger, the fight changed dramatically. The wolfhound loosened its jaws slightly, and Black Tiger swiftly bit down on one of the wolfhound's front legs. José's dog howled, then quickly sprang into the air as it retreated.

Before Black Tiger had the chance to turn around, a new opponent emerged. Arturo's sheepdog jumped forward like a bolt of white lightning and pulled Black Tiger under its body. The wolfhound took a moment to catch its breath and then jumped back into the fight. The two bigger dogs and Black Tiger all rolled around in a ball.

Alex's pug rushed forward to join in the commotion. It excitedly ran circles around the three dogs, barking with high-pitched yaps, as if celebrating the wolfhound and sheepdog's victory – or mocking Black Tiger for his defeat.

By the time the three dogs swaggered away, Black Tiger was lying, still, on the ground. Pedro picked up his pup and couldn't help crying out when he saw the injuries covering his body. 'Black Tiger, you can't die! You have to live!' Pedro cried. 'I'll train you, and we can be strong together! Black Tiger, you can't die ...'

Pedro comforted Black Tiger while he wept, but Black Tiger appeared very calm, and looked at the boy with glittering black eyes, as if to say, 'I'm fine – please don't cry.'

It only took Black Tiger a few days to recover, and Pedro really did start training him — how to lie down, sit, jump over obstacles and search for hidden things. Black Tiger was very clever and learnt quickly. He also had a great memory and never forgot a trick. When the pup was tired from training, Pedro would stop to give him a piece of bread and some water.

Pedro and Old Juan didn't have much money, so Black Tiger ate whatever they ate. There was bread, potatoes, cornbread, and sometimes beef and chicken. Black Tiger would always eat with relish. He wasn't picky at all. But whenever they left home, he didn't touch a single thing. He didn't even look at food that he saw on the side of the road. Of course, this was because of Pedro's training. He had once seen a film about a police dog, and those clever police dogs never touched any food that strangers gave them.

Pedro trained Black Tiger in private. It was his secret – he couldn't let José and the others know about it. If they found out, they would probably laugh at him again. But Pedro truly believed that one day Black Tiger would show them all how special he was.

One morning, Pedro and Black Tiger were at the bottom of the stairs when they came face to face with José and his big dog. José stuck his head up and started whistling, pleased with himself. He even deliberately pulled his big dog close to Black Tiger. The wolfhound growled threateningly, baring his white teeth. Pedro pretended not to mind, but he felt nervous. If José loosened his grip and let his wolfhound leap up, Black Tiger would be on the losing side of the fight.

But, strangely, Black Tiger didn't seem to care at all. Faced with the larger dog, who eyed him menacingly, Black Tiger didn't pull back. He even took a big step forward, his eyes glowing with a warm light. From then on, whenever he saw that wolfhound, this was how Black Tiger dealt with it – with no fear and no resentment.

Pedro thought it was a bit unusual. One night, as they were all having supper, Pedro patted Black Tiger's head and asked quietly, 'Hey, Tiger. Sometimes I just don't understand you. Do you feel fear at all?

Black Tiger lifted his head and looked at Pedro with those piercing eyes.

Old Juan started chuckling. 'Silly boy! You really think that dog can understand you? Whatever next!'

Moments later, without warning, Black Tiger made a loud howling noise. He squirmed out of Pedro's arms and bolted towards the door. He butted it with his head, then anxiously began running circles around the room and panting.

'What are you looking for, Black Tiger?' Pedro asked in surprise.

Black Tiger ignored him. Instead he crouched at the door, his entire body quivering.

Pedro sprang up and wrenched open the door. There was no one there.

'That's weird,' Pedro said, closing the door. 'What's wrong with Black Tiger?'

Old Juan turned off the lights and said, 'He must be upset. It's fine. Go to sleep now.'

In the darkness, Black Tiger's panting became more and more annoying. *What is wrong with him?* Pedro wondered.

Pedro gradually drifted off to sleep. Even in his dreams he could hear Black Tiger's panting. It sounded like a swarm of wasps that was flying far away then coming straight back. Finally, the wasps stopped flying and began dancing around him, even more frenzied, as if they might drown him, or even eat him. Ouch! The back of his hand was stung by a wasp …

Pedro cried out and jumped off his bed. He rubbed the back of his hand and looked around with panicked eyes, but there wasn't a single wasp in the room. As he was trying to figure out what had happened, he felt a stab of pain in his foot, and he looked down to see Black Tiger biting it! Pedro was furious. *This pup is really going crazy!* he thought. He lifted his hand to smack Black Tiger, but it hung in the air. He couldn't go through with it.

It was Black Tiger's gaze that stopped Pedro. He was staring at the boy with fear, anxiety and a sorrowful pleading in his eyes. He looked at Pedro for some time, then suddenly jumped onto him, bit his sleeve and pulled at him, growling as he struggled to drag Pedro towards the door.

Old Juan rolled out of bed. He grabbed Black Tiger and pushed him outside, yelling, 'You silly little thing! You've kept me up all night, and you still want to mess around? Get out of here!'

Surprisingly, as soon as Black Tiger's feet hit the ground, he bolted into the room again. Biting Pedro's trouser legs so they began to tear, Black Tiger dragged Pedro outside their apartment. Old Juan followed, muttering furiously, 'This pup really must be crazy!'

As soon as Pedro reached the entrance to the apartment building, the concrete beneath his feet suddenly – unbelievably – began to shake. For a moment he thought that he was still asleep and dreaming, but the ground began shaking more and more violently until he fell down with a thud, unable to stand upright. Looking behind him, he saw his grandpa had fallen too. The concrete rocked up and down, like the deck of a ship sailing through a storm. Old Juan sat on the ground for a few seconds, stunned, then cried out in alarm: 'Earthquake! It's an earthquake!'

Pedro looked up, and what he saw was like something from a film. The square outside was rolling in waves like the surface of a lake. The buildings around the square looked like crazed people of different heights, shaking where they stood, as if they were trying to free themselves from the earth. In the distance, some larger buildings had split in half, crumbling and shaking, then had disappeared in clouds of dust. The TV tower was still standing, tall and majestic, but it was shaking more severely than any other building. After a few shudders back and forth, it could no longer support itself and slowly tumbled down. Terrifying cracking sounds split the air from near and far. Some of the blasts were deafening.

Pedro couldn't help crying out in shock: 'Oh! Oh my god!'

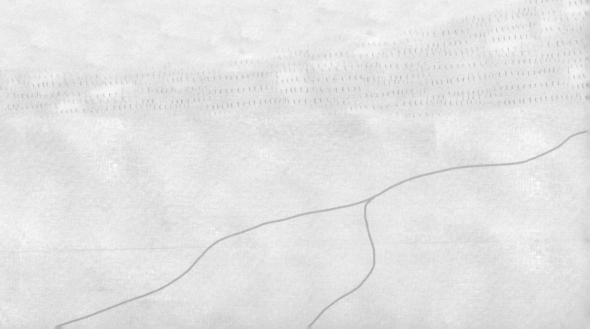

The twelve storeys of the New Leon Apartments looked like a tall chest of drawers that someone had thrown up into the sky. Shaking frantically, the apartments tossed their broken windows and cracked concrete out into the air. The yellow and grey walls cracked open as if they had been split by bolts of lightning, and the cracks quickly became terrifying snakes that crawled up the walls, spreading and spreading …

Pedro was looking around, not knowing what to do, when Old Juan jumped up, grabbed Pedro's collar and ran towards the empty square as fast as he could. The two stumbled a dozen or so steps. All they could hear were the echoes of the collapsing buildings – it was like an avalanche. As they turned and looked back, they saw that the towering New Leon Apartments were gone, and in their place was a huge pile of concrete, tiles and bricks, enveloped in a big cloud of smoke. The New Leon Apartments were gone forever.

After a while, the earth stopped shaking. Pedro hugged his grandpa tightly as the two stood in a daze. Black Tiger was curled up next to Pedro's foot, staring dumbly at the fallen apartment building. A horrible silence fell around them, like the calm that comes just before a volcano erupts. After ten seconds or so, terrible sounds started coming from the collapsed building: cries for help, weeping, moaning ... The sounds seemed to be coming from somewhere deep below the earth. *How many people have lost their lives in this mountain of tiles and bricks? How many are still alive? How many have been injured?* So many questions ran through Pedro's mind.

Old Juan lowered his head, and slowly kneeled down. There were so many people he had greeted every day in that building, and now they were buried. It was hard to believe. Tears rolled down his dusty cheeks.

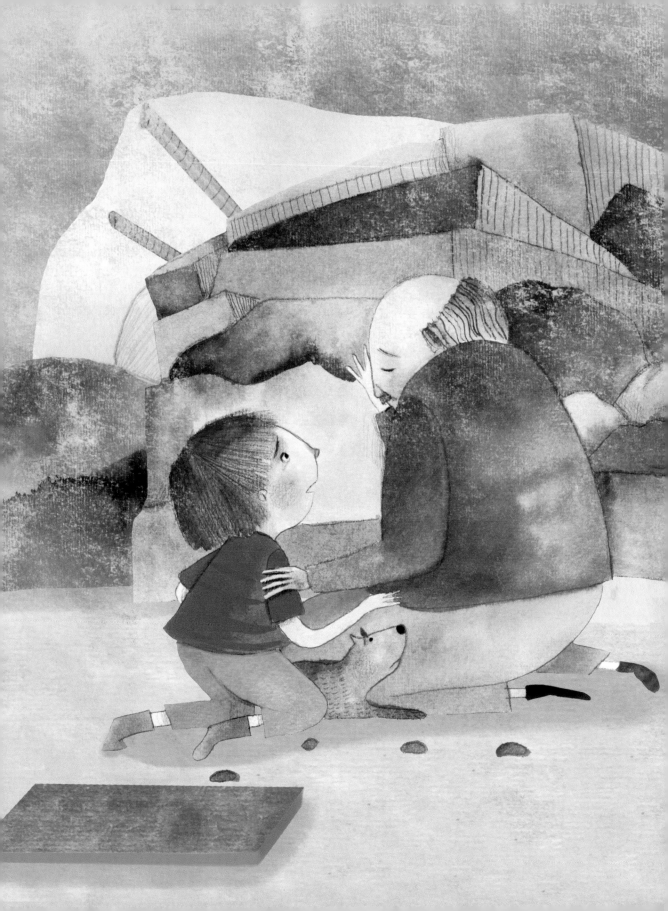

Pedro hugged Black Tiger close to his chest and sobbed silently. Everything had happened so quickly that he still couldn't understand it. But there was one thing he was sure of: if it hadn't been for Black Tiger, he and his grandpa would have been buried underneath the building. Black Tiger had saved their lives, but how had Black Tiger known about the earthquake? It was a mystery.

Of all the buildings around them, the New Leon Apartments were the most severely damaged. Elderly people were kneeling on the ground, weeping. Mothers who couldn't find their children were beating their chests and stamping their feet in despair. Men with tear-streaked faces were desperately clawing at the pile of rubble. And some people were just numb with fear – they sat woodenly on the ground, with looks of hopelessness on their faces …

Among the panic-stricken people in the square, Pedro discovered José's mother and father. José's mother was leaning on her husband's shoulder, sobbing. José's father was wearing his police uniform but he had lost his proud, dignified manner. There were tears in his eyes as he stroked his wife's shoulders and quietly consoled her …

It appeared that José was buried in the rubble. His wolfhound hadn't been able to find him. Pedro saw that freckled face appear in front of him again, with its mocking gaze. He had once hated that face, but at this moment, faced with José's poor mother and his father, all the hate he had gathered up inside him dissolved. *Could José still be alive under all that rubble?* he wondered.

People slowly came crawling out of the collapsed building. These survivors didn't care that they were covered in dirt and blood. They just held their families and cried with a mix of joy and pain. Some people were calling out for help from beneath the rubble but couldn't manage to crawl out.

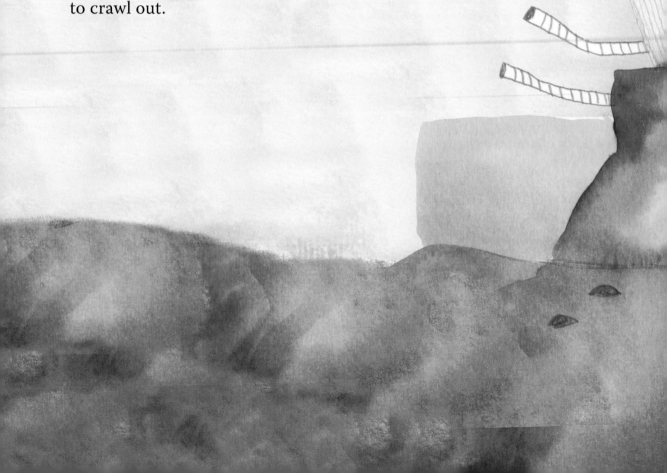

Pedro suddenly had an idea. *Could he get Black Tiger to crawl into the rubble to save people?* he thought. He had trained Black Tiger to find hidden things before, and the clever dog had been able to do it every time. He crouched down and gently patted Black Tiger's back, then gave him a command like he did during training: 'Go, Black Tiger! Go!' With a wag of his tail, Black Tiger jumped onto the rubble, climbing up to a high spot. He then quickly disappeared into a crack.

Just then, several police cars drove up with their sirens wailing. A crowd of police officers jumped out of the cars to maintain order, blocking off the streets near the New Leon Apartments and directing people away. Old Juan was told to leave by the officers. A tall policeman grabbed hold of Pedro's collar and tried to pull him away, but Pedro screamed, 'Let me go! My Black Tiger is saving people, and he's not out yet! Let me stay! Let me stay!'

Perhaps Pedro's shouts had made the police officer curious, because he put Pedro down and asked him loudly, 'What black tiger? What are you talking about?'

'Black Tiger is my dog. He saved me and my grandpa today! He's in there saving other people right now. It's true, I'm not lying!'

The policeman didn't ask any more questions, but he let Pedro go and moved away to other groups of people, telling them to leave the area. Pedro went back to the rubble and climbed in the direction Black Tiger had climbed. He found the hole that Black Tiger had crawled into, then cupped his hands around his mouth and called out, 'Black Tiger! Black Tiger! Cooooome ooooout!'

After fifteen long minutes, Black Tiger finally emerged from the hole. He came out tail-first, slowly working his way up while dragging a big bag. It took Black Tiger a lot of effort to drag the bag up. Underneath the sound of his panting, Pedro could faintly hear a high-pitched noise. It kept starting and stopping and sounded like a cat.

Only then did Pedro clearly see that the bag was not a bag at all. Black Tiger had saved a baby! The infant, tightly swaddled in a blanket, did not have a single mark on him, and he was crying so hard that his eyes were closed. But poor Black Tiger had scratches all over his body from the jagged steel bars in the rubble.

Members of the rescue team gathered around them. The baby was passed down the line, but nobody claimed him. He was taken to the local hospital along with the injured.

Soon Black Tiger became the hero of the rescue team. He would sniff around the rubble, and when he stopped moving and began to bark at the ground, the rescue workers would rush forward, moving aside bricks, pulling up concrete and even bringing in a crane to push aside the bigger blocks they couldn't move with their hands. When they discovered a wounded survivor, the crowd couldn't help cheering for joy. But Black Tiger would already be somewhere else, looking for more injured people.

After many tiring hours, Black Tiger had helped the rescue workers save five injured people. He was exhausted, and his coat was covered in dirt and scratches.

Pedro really couldn't bear to see Black Tiger like that and hugged him tightly. He fed him a sausage, gave him some water and gently tended to the cuts and grazes all over his body. The food and water had been brought over by the tall police officer who had tried to get Pedro to leave. He clapped Pedro on the shoulder and said with a smile, 'Well done, kid! You did us a huge favour. Give your pup his reward.' As Pedro and Black Tiger walked around the square, people made way for them.

Many more people were dug out of the rubble. Some were injured very badly. Among the victims, Pedro discovered Arturo and Alex. Arturo's sheepdog was alive, but one of its legs had been broken. Pedro felt so sad.

José still hadn't been found, and there was no sign of his wolfhound either. Could they still be alive?

José's home had been on the second floor of the building, so it was at the very bottom of the rubble. It would be a miracle if anyone on that floor was still alive. But how would they know if anyone had survived down there?

Soon after the earthquake, José's father had bravely begun to help direct the rescue – even though he didn't know if his own son was dead or alive. He stood on a large bit of concrete, waving his hands and shouting instructions, his black uniform covered in dust. José's mother sat on a rock, staring into space. Every time someone was pulled from the rubble, she would stand up excitedly. But time after time she was disappointed. Her red, swollen eyes had run out of tears, and all she could do was stare at the mountain of debris in front of her. Pedro noticed that she had a bright-red jumper and a backpack with her, and he knew right away that they belonged to José. In that instant, he thought of a way he could help.

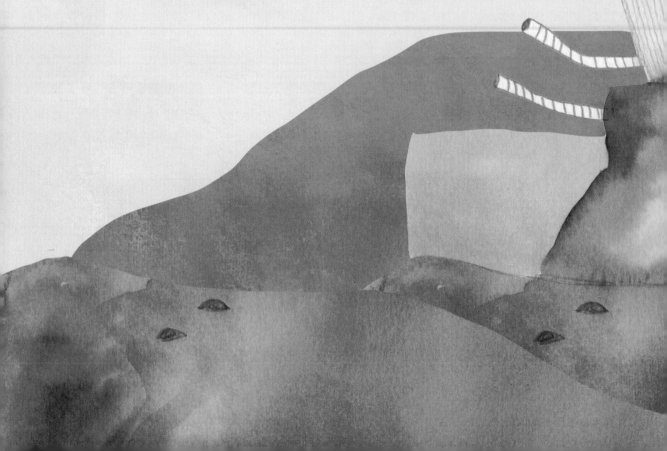

Pedro brought Black Tiger over to stand in front of José's mother, and said softly, 'I can help you, ma'am.'

José's mother looked up at Pedro, looking confused.

He spoke again. 'Would you let me borrow José's jumper and backpack, please? I can use them to help you find him.'

José's mother's eyes lit up, and she asked in amazement, 'What did you say? You have a way to save him?' She didn't know Pedro, and didn't know that her son had bullied him. She couldn't believe that this boy, who was covered in dirt, could produce a miracle.

Pedro patted Black Tiger's head and said earnestly, 'Let's try. Black Tiger can help me. He's already saved a few people today!' Black Tiger looked up at José's mother with his glittering eyes.

José's mother hesitated, then handed the jumper and backpack to Pedro. Pedro opened up José's backpack, took out a pen, tore off a blank page from a notebook and scrawled three lines:

José, are you hurt?
We're trying to find a way to save you!
Please write back!

He folded the paper into a long strip, then found a thin cord and wrapped the pen and paper together around Black Tiger's neck. He let Black Tiger smell José's jumper and backpack. Black Tiger was calm, as if he understood everything that was going on.

'Black Tiger, go and find José! Go on, boy!' As soon as Pedro issued the command, Black Tiger leapt into the rubble. With a few more jumps, he disappeared.

José's mother stood up, gazing in the direction Black Tiger had gone. A speck of hope appeared in her anxious eyes.

Each minute passed extremely slowly. Pedro sat on the ground, rubbing his hair in frustration. If only he could look through the concrete and bricks to see where Black Tiger had gone. José's mother was even more restless. She wanted to dive into the rubble to look for him herself.

After half an hour, Black Tiger still hadn't returned. José's mother tapped Pedro on the shoulder and nervously asked, 'Do you think your pup ran off?'

'Never!' Pedro said bluntly.
'Does your pup know José?'
Pedro silently nodded his head.
'You and José are good friends?'
Pedro was surprised by the question and didn't know how to respond.
If he told the truth, he was worried José's mother would be shocked, and
would worry even more. But he wasn't good at lying.

Before he could answer, Pedro heard Black Tiger's barks coming from the rubble. José's mother and Pedro turned around and saw Black Tiger running towards them, with the pen and paper still around his neck!

Pedro's hands trembled as he undid Black Tiger's collar. He thought that the paper seemed different, as if it had been opened by someone. He was just about to open up the note when José's mother reached out and snatched it away.

Tears started streaming down her face, and she began to laugh and cry at the same time. 'Oh, my José!' she cried softly, and buried her head in the note.

Pedro took the note from her. Underneath the words he had written was another line:

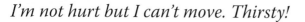

I'm not hurt but I can't move. Thirsty!

'José is still alive!'

José's mother yelled out and ran to her husband. His eyes grew red as he read the note. He grabbed Pedro's hand and said, 'Thank you, boy!'

'Thank me for what? José hasn't been saved yet!' Pedro answered.

Jose's father thought for a moment, then ripped another sheet of paper out of the notebook, wrote something down and gave the paper to Pedro, saying, 'Please ask your pup to take another message to José!' Before Pedro could even read the note, José's mother wrenched it out of his hands and wrote another line. Pedro read it:

My dear son, hang in there. We're coming to get you! Your mother and I are with you!

Papa

We love you! Don't be scared!

Mama

Pedro picked up the pen, then added:

Black Tiger and I are your friends now.

Pedro

The note and pen were tied together, then attached to Black Tiger's neck again. Pedro also found a water bottle, filled it with water and attached that to the cord too.

'Good boy, Black Tiger! You can do it again!' Pedro patted Black Tiger's grazed body. The water bottle around Black Tiger's neck made it harder for him to move, but he was still brimming with energy. He dived into the rubble without even looking back.

José's father immediately gathered a rescue squad. They moved rubble aside, and worked for a long time, but they barely seemed to make any progress. Each huge piece of concrete weighed many tons and couldn't be moved by human hands. Besides, if they weren't careful, the slabs of concrete and stacks of bricks would tumble down, endangering the lives of the survivors below. The crane helped, picking up one slab at a time, but progress was extremely slow.

Black Tiger didn't come out for more than half an hour. When he did, he had new scratches all over him and looked exhausted. The bottle attached to his neck had been taken, and on the back of the note was José's handwriting:

Papa and Mama: I'll wait for you! I love you!

Pedro: Thank you and Black Tiger. I'm sorry for what I did to you!

By now, it was nearly dusk. When night fell, the rescue work would become even harder. After a while, the rescue team found more concrete blocking their path. If any of the slabs moved, the rest of the rubble could collapse. Eventually the rescue team stopped work.

With her face streaked with tears, José's mother fell down on her knees in front of the rescue workers. But there was nothing they could do. José's father lost his composure, and began hoarsely yelling José's name towards the rubble …

Pedro patted Black Tiger's head, and silently looked at everything in front of him. José's face appeared in his mind, and it was a face filled with hope. *José, José*, Pedro thought. *You have to hang in there!*

Black Tiger, who had remained quiet, now began barking peculiarly at the bricks, as if he had discovered a secret. Pedro grew tense. *Has something happened to José?* he wondered. Before he knew what was happening, Black Tiger had pulled himself free from Pedro's arms and dived into the rubble. This time, he barked as he crawled forward into the crack, and slowly, his barks grew fainter and fainter. *What is Black Tiger doing?* Pedro thought.

José's mother and father also saw Black Tiger jump under the concrete. They thought it was a bad omen. They hugged each other tightly, and nervously listened to Black Tiger's intermittent barking as it faded away.

One minute passed, then thirty, then forty-five, and Black Tiger still hadn't come back. The sky was growing darker, but the rescue squad didn't leave. They too were worried. Was José dead or alive?

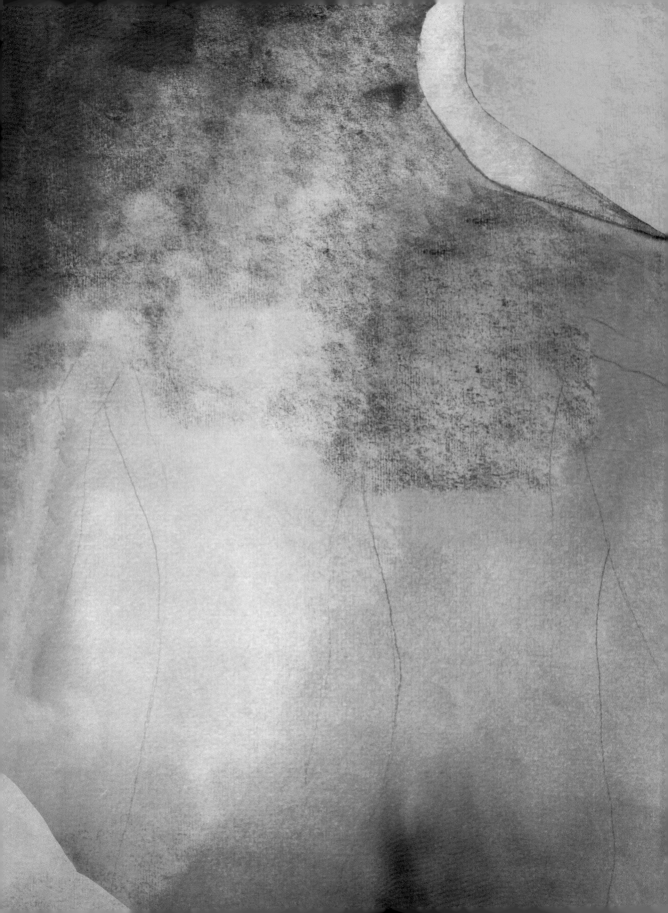

Pedro climbed onto the rubble and began yelling at the top of his lungs down the hole where Black Tiger had disappeared, 'Black Tiger! Black Tiger!' The sound travelled a long way down, and echoed, but he couldn't hear Black Tiger's barking. Pedro kept yelling. He was sure that Black Tiger would be able to hear his voice.

Then, from deep inside the rubble, he heard Black Tiger's bark. The sound was weak, as if Black Tiger was having trouble breathing. The people standing below Pedro heard it too. José's father climbed up to stand with Pedro at the hole in the rubble.

Black Tiger's barks grew louder and louder as he slowly approached the surface. Would José be with him? Pedro yelled a few times, and miraculously, José's voice answered him! It wasn't far from the surface. 'Black Tiger is bringing me out!' José called. 'I can see the light! I ...'

Before José had finished, Pedro heard a rumbling and felt the earth shaking fiercely under his feet. It was an aftershock. He and José's father both fell down. Pedro heard a horrible yelp from somewhere beneath him, but it was immediately followed by silence.

José's father went pale. *How would José make it up to the surface now?* he despaired.

The rescue team rushed forward, moving pieces of cracked concrete as quickly as they could. Soon they could hear José sobbing. He was alive! But he was trapped …

Dozens of people worked together to move the concrete, finally revealing José lying unhurt on his side. Black Tiger was lying completely still next to him. Pedro rushed to Black Tiger's side and began to weep.

José hugged his parents and cried. 'It was Black Tiger who saved me,' he sobbed. 'If he hadn't pulled on my shirt to show me the way, there's no way I would have made it up here.'

It was only then that everyone remembered Black Tiger and Pedro. But Pedro was nowhere to be seen, and Black Tiger's body had disappeared too.

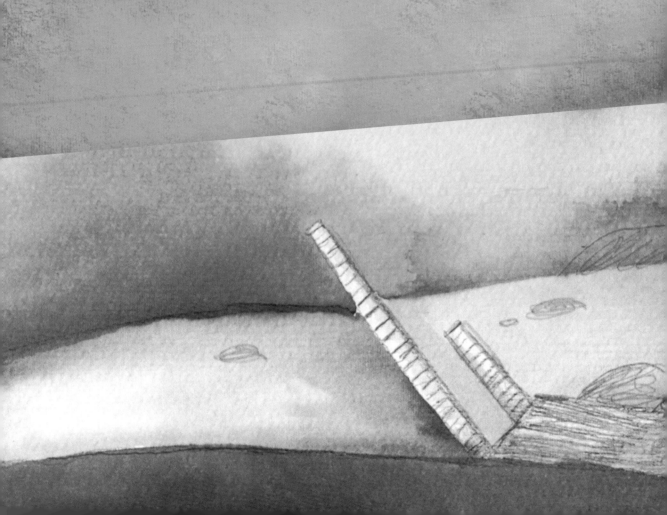

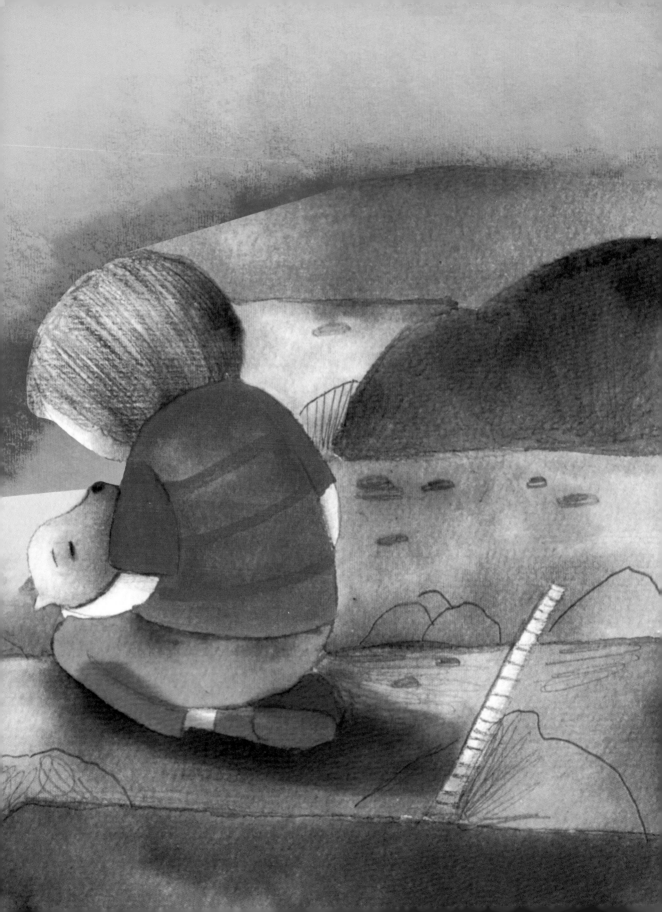

Several days later, someone discovered a small wooden plaque in the Dolores Cemetery in Mexico City, with these words on it:

HERE LIES MAN'S BEST FRIEND – BLACK TIGER.
IN A TRAGIC EARTHQUAKE, HE SACRIFICED HIS LIFE FOR HUMANS.
WE WILL ALWAYS REMEMBER HIM.

If you ever visit that cemetery on the anniversary of the earthquake, you will see two children and an old man standing in front of the little wooden plaque, their heads bowed in deep respect.